SEEING RED

HarperFestival is an imprint of HarperCollins Publishers.

The Angry Birds™ Movie: Seeing Red
© 2016 Rovio Animation Ltd., Angry Birds, and all related properties, titles, logos, and characters are trademarks
of Rovio Entertainment Ltd. and Rovio Animation Ltd. and are used with permission. All rights reserved.
Printed in the United States of America.
No part of this book may be used or reproduced in any manner whatsoever without written permission except
in the case of brief quotations embodied in critical articles and reviews. For information address HarperCollins
Children's Books, a division of HarperCollins Publishers, 195 Broadway, New York, NY 10007.
www.harpercollinschildrens.com

ISBN 978-0-06-245338-9

16 17 18 19 20   CWM   10 9 8 7 6 5 4 3 2 1
❖
First Edition

THE ANGRY BIRDS™ MOVIE

SEEING RED

Illustrations by Tuğrul Karacan
Based on a story written by Sarah Stephens

HARPER FESTIVAL
An Imprint of HarperCollins*Publishers*

It was a beautiful day on Bird Island—the kind of day that got a bird chirping, unless that bird was Red, who always started the day angry.

Red loved the hut he'd built on the quiet beach. He had big plans to make it even better. So when a flock of construction workers drilling outside his hut woke him up, he fumed. He went outside to complain, but the bird delivering the newspaper hit him in the head. Red was so mad, he forgot about breakfast.

Red headed into town for a meeting. First he stopped at Bird on a Wire Café. He needed to adjust his attitude. A snack would help. But the coffee was cold, the seedcake was stale, and the chatty waiter got on his last nerve. Red stormed off.

Red met with Prudence. Her job was to help birds find work. She and Red met regularly. His bad temper caused him to be fired . . . a lot. Deep down, Prudence knew Red was a good egg. She was determined to find the right fit for him.

"There are too many bird-brained birds out there!" Red ranted about his last job.

"Try not to fly off the handle," Prudence said. She told him about a new job. He could start the next day.

The following morning Red arrived at Early Bird Worms. They sold the plumpest, tastiest worms and were always busy. Red helped fill the takeout orders. He rushed to count the wriggly worms but could not keep up with the steady stream of customers.

"Step on it!" his boss bellowed.

Red dropped the order he was filling and
did exactly what his boss told him to do.

"You're fired!" she shouted.

Red stomped straight over to Prudence's office. She couldn't believe her eyes.

Still, Prudence would not give up. She found Red a job at Late Riser Worms. It was the same work as the job at Early Bird's but less hectic. Red needed to relax.

The next morning Red arrived ready to work. But the boss was asleep and there were no customers—which was a good thing, since there were no worms to sell!

The delivery bird explained, "It doesn't matter. The shop next door, Early Bird, always gets the worms."

Except it mattered to Red. He wanted to work. He needed money to finish his hut. Red's squawking woke the boss, just in time for Red to quit.

Prudence persevered. She found a job for Red at the Nap Bar, one of the most relaxing places on Bird Island.

The next morning Red learned how to load birds into rest-nests. Once the nests were full, Red could nap, too. Sleeping on the job sounded like a dream. Plus, Red couldn't get mad if he was asleep.

Red filled the nests with drowsy birds and then climbed into his own rest-nest and drifted off to sleep.

HHOONNGKKKSHU . .

CHRRAARRRRR-PBPBPBP!

HRACCHH-SHWEEEEE . . .

What was that awful noise?

Red discovered the source. The napping birds were snoring!

Red shook and shushed the noisy snorers. As soon as one bird quieted down, another started making a racket.

"This isn't a dream job. It's a nightmare!" he yelled.

The birds woke up angry—just like Red, who was promptly fired.

Prudence was done and so was her job list.

"I'll take anything!" Red pleaded.

Prudence remembered one last job—a job everyone hated.

"You'll have to deliver cakes to bird-day parties and entertain the guests and wear a costume," she said.

As long as he could fix up his hut, Red didn't care. He started immediately.

Red looked funny in the crazy getup. He looked so funny that when he saw his reflection in the window he almost laughed himself!

"This might just be my best job yet! What could possibly go wrong?" Red said.

Prudence had to agree, but she was laughing too hard to speak.